THE BAD MOOD MONSTER

Authored by C.D. White

Illustrated by Jean Adamov

Creative Creatures Publishing

Imagine. Explore. Create.

THIS BOOK BELONGS TO:

_____

For Kaleb and Antoinette,
my love and inspiration.
C.D.W.

For my children and
all the bad mood monsters.
J.A.

Mansfield Malcolm Marcus White

was in a terrible mood last Tuesday night.

His mother said,

"Manny, why such a scowl?

With a look like that,

I'd expect you to howl."

"A bad mood can be a horrible sight,

it can turn some of us into monsters overnight."

Manny just frowned and put his nose in the air,

"I don't believe you, and if it did happen, I wouldn't care."

His mom threw her hands up as she walked away.

Manny called after her,

"I'm not in a bad mood today!"

Manny's sister Annabelle was in his room playing.

Upon seeing this he crossed his arms, saying,

"Out of my room.

In here, you're not staying!"

She hung her head low as she put down his toys.

"Play in your own room!"

said Manny's growling voice.

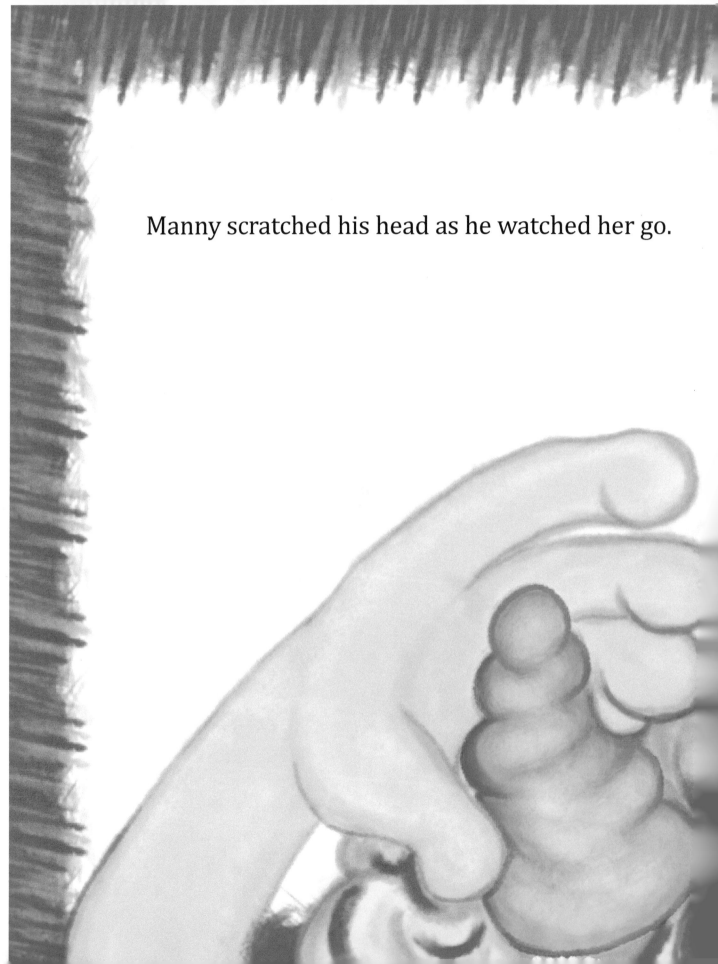

Manny scratched his head as he watched her go.

She did not look up to see his horns grow.

Two twisted, green, horns

sprouted on top of his head.

He looked in the mirror. His hair had turned red.

"This just won't do, these horns cannot stay.

This makes me so mad. I want them to go away!"

But the horns stayed put,

and his bad mood didn't change.

Would he be allowed in school,

looking so strange?

As Manny stomped his way down the hall,

a long spiked tail from his backside did fall.

"And now what is this?" he yelled,

waving the tail about.

"I am so MAD!"

was all he could shout.

His father said,

"Mansfield, what's all the huff?"

Manny opened his mouth to answer,

and out floated a smoke puff.

"A puff of smoke, that's not much.

A flame,

now that would be some big stuff!"

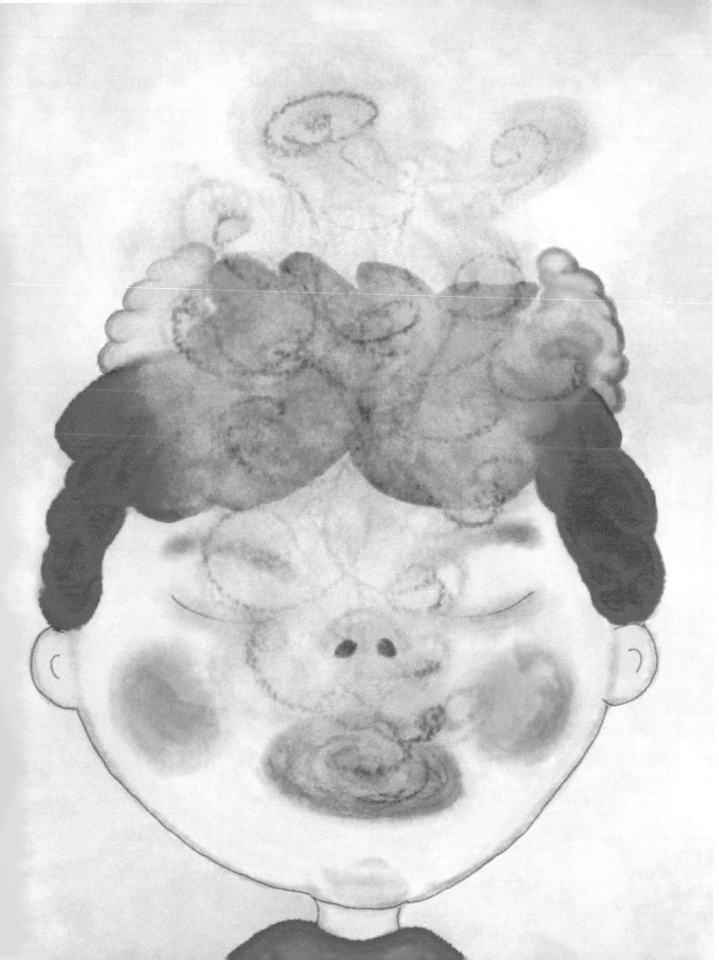

As Manny kicked, his poor dog's toy bone,

a huge burst of fire, from his mouth, was blown.

"Manny, it's time for dinner," his mother said.

He thought,

"this is no time for eating,"

and ran to his bed.

Manny's father came knocking

on the bedroom door,

"Will you join us at the table?"

With a new pair of horns,

flaming breath, and a tail,

Manny did not feel he was able.

"I'm not hungry," he yelled through the door,

"and I'm not coming out."

His father said, sadly,

"Then in your room, you can stay,

where you can feel free to pout."

Angry with his new monster appearance,

Manny thrashed around his room,

causing a huge disturbance.

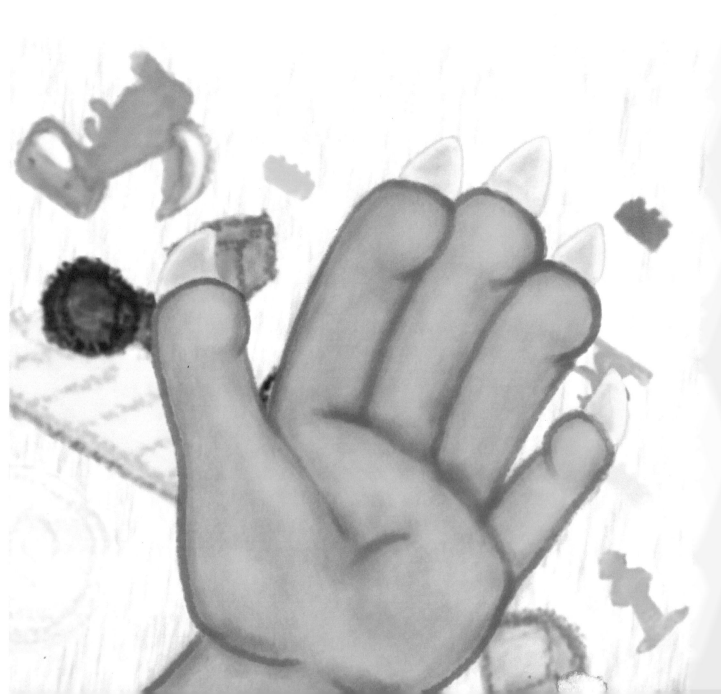

When he thought nothing could be any worse,

his hands turned to claws!

He moaned, "What a curse!"

He waited for his family to fall asleep

and out to the kitchen, he quietly sneaked.

"I'm starving," Manny said to himself.

He grabbed a bag of pretzels

from the pantry shelf.

Manny pulled at the bag to open the treat,

with his clumsy claws, this was no easy feat.

Finally, with new fangs and an angry crunch,

Manny was ready for pretzels to munch.

After Manny devoured the snack,

a sleepy monster decided to hit the sack.

He tossed, and he turned, he couldn't get comfy,

the spikes down his back felt rather lumpy.

"What will Annabelle say with me as her brother?"

"I shouldn't be grouchy.

I should have listened to Mother."

"I really need sleep," he said with a sigh.

"I'll be nicer tomorrow, at least I will try."

He closed his big gray monster eyes,

dreaming a hopeful dream.

When he awoke in the morning

he no longer felt mean.

He looked at his hands,

and the claws were not there.

He felt for the horns

and found only hair.

No more flame-throwing breath,

or tail on his behind.

Mansfield could start anew,

today he would be kind.

He leapt from his bed

and flung open the door.

"Annabelle," he called,

"I've changed,

I won't be grouchy anymore."

But instead of her sweet voice

answering back,

A beast with pigtails appeared

ready to attack.

Manny said, "Who is this monster?"

He could not tell.

It's not a ferocious beast,

it is a grouchy Annabelle!

C.D. White

has always loved making up stories, first for her younger sister and then for her two children. She has a strong creative background, including graphic design, muralist, and currently, she is designing jewelry, as well as making up more stories. When she is not creating, she enjoys spending time with her family, especially her husband Mark, who has always supported her creativity.

Jean Adamov

has authored and illustrated
The LJJ Adventures
a series of children's books based on the adventures of her three children. Her family is her inspiration and joy. She has always loved art and creating children's books has become a wonderful way to share exciting stories with others. She is pleased to be collaborating with C.D. White on this amazing project.

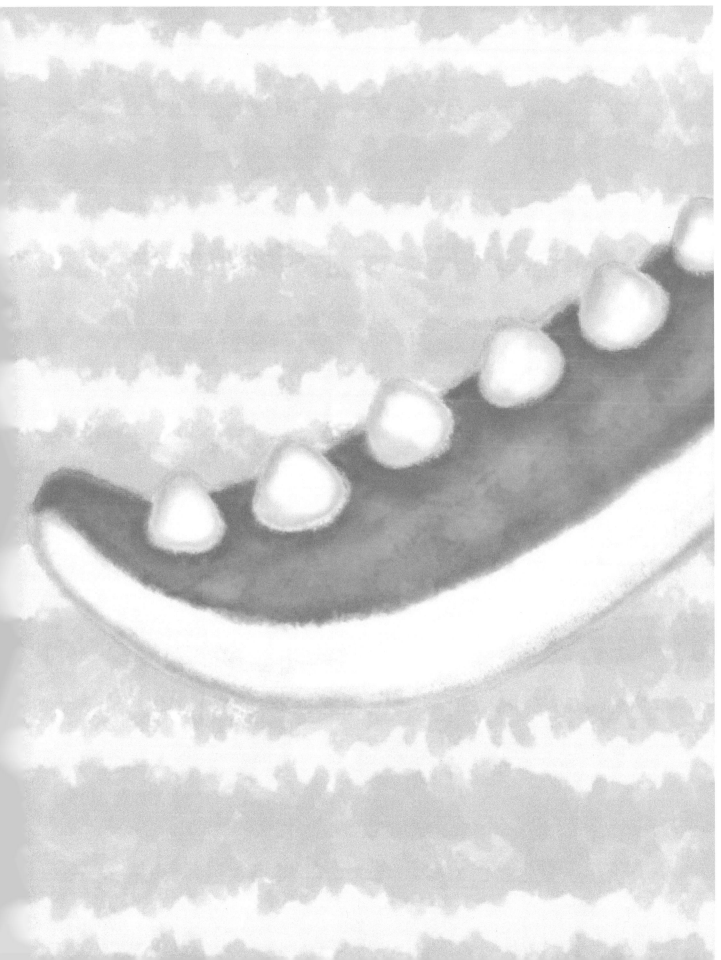

CPSIA information can be obtained
at www.ICGtesting.com
Printed in the USA
BVHW021344081120
592580BV00005B/28